PRINCESS CHAMOMILE
Gets Her Way

Hiawyn Oram

illustrated by
Susan Varley

DUTTON CHILDREN'S BOOKS · NEW YORK

For Lara, with love—H.O.

For Princess M and Princess C
(and their mum and dad)—S.V.

Text copyright © 1998 by Hiawyn Oram
Illustrations copyright © 1998 by Susan Varley

CIP Data is available.

Published in the United States 1999 by Dutton Children's Books,
a division of Penguin Putnam Books for Young Readers,
345 Hudson Street, New York, New York 10014
http://www.penguinputnam.com/yreaders/index.htm

Originally published in Great Britain 1998 by Andersen Press, Ltd., London
Typography by Alan Carr
Printed in Italy
First American Edition
ISBN 0-525-46148-5
2 4 6 8 10 9 7 5 3 1

Chamomile was a princess with a problem. Her nanny, Nanny Nettle, didn't allow *this*; she didn't allow *that*. She didn't allow Chamomile to go without her tiara or wear old clothes, or ride her new bike beyond the castle walls. And Nanny Nettle *never* allowed Chamomile to eat sweets — not even at her own birthday parties!

One morning, Princess Chamomile woke up early and said, "Enough is enough! I'm tired of being a Not-Allowed!" She pulled on some old shorts and a T-shirt.

She crept past Nanny Nettle's room.

She ran behind the gardener's back and got out her bike. Then she opened the secret door in the castle wall . . .

and pedaled out into the big wide world.

"Now," she said, "all I need is a candy store!"

And as soon as she turned a corner, there it was—Bags-Eye the Bad Cat's Candy Store. Inside, Bags-Eye was stroking his greasy whiskers over his greasy newspaper and wondering, not for the first time, how bad a bad cat could be.

"Do *you* know?" he purred in his greasy purr as Chamomile stepped into the shop.

"Know what?" asked Chamomile.

"How bad a bad cat can be?" purred Bags-Eye.

"If you want to be bad, eat a lot of these," said Chamomile, pointing at all the sweets. "They're not allowed."

"Oh, but they are allowed! As many as you like, if you can pay for them," purred Bags-Eye. "Here's a bag!"

"Thank you," said Chamomile, taking the bag. "But I can't pay for anything. I'm a princess, you know, and I'm never allowed to handle money!"

"A princess?" Bags-Eye's greasy purr grew even greasier. "In that case, my dear, here's . . . *another bag!*"

And with a well-practiced swirl, he threw the sack over Chamomile, pulled the drawstring, swung her over his shoulder, and bundled her upstairs.

Meanwhile, back at the castle, everyone had woken up to find Princess Chamomile missing. The queen was screaming, "*Where is she?*"

"I c-c-can't think," stammered Nanny Nettle.

"She's never allowed to . . ."

"Well, it looks as if she's done it anyway!" yelled the king. "Call the gardener! Call everyone! Search everywhere! House, grounds, and *especially* where she's not allowed!"

While the royal search party searched, Bags-Eye rubbed his greasy paws together and untied Chamomile's sack.

"Now," he said, "all we have to do is write your father a ransom note demanding loads of money for you. Then I'll be bad *and* rich. Yippee!"

"*We?*" asked Chamomile. "Can't you write?"

"When would I have learned to write?

"Or read, for that matter," snarled Bags-Eye. "I've been far too busy studying to be bad. Now . . . I'll dictate! You'll write!"

"Hmm," said Chamomile thoughtfully. "All right. On one condition: for every word I write, I get one of what I'm not allowed."

"Sure," said Bags-Eye, shrugging. "Why should I care if all your teeth fall out? Let's get on with it."

So Chamomile sat on the floor with paper and pen. "Go ahead," she said happily.

"Dear King Waldo," dictated Bags-Eye, pacing back and forth.

Dear Daddy wrote Chamomile cleverly.

"I have your precious daughter," dictated Bags-Eye.

I'm at a place where I'm not allowed called Bags-Eye's Candy Store wrote Chamomile.

"If you want her back, leave a huge amount of money outside the castle gates at midnight, and I'll drop her off at dawn. Sincerely yours, No-One-You-Know," dictated Bags-Eye.

But I'm enjoying myself, so don't come and get me for half an hour.
Lots of love,
C. XXXXX

wrote Chamomile.

Then she and Bags-Eye counted up all the words in the note. While Bags-Eye set off to slip it under the castle door, Chamomile went downstairs to the shop and chose . . .

. . . *three* sugar bears, *four* jelly mice, *two* licorice wheels, *one* pack of blueberry gum, *two* sherbet dibdabs, *one* chocolate bunny, *four* marzipan roses, *two* sugarplums, *four* nougat-nut whirls, *two* cherry balls, and *seven* candied almonds.

And by the time the king had received the note and roared for the queen, who roared for Nanny Nettle . . .

who roared for the gardener, who roared for the chauffeur . . .

. . . and they'd all roared down the road, nearly running over Bags-Eye . . .

. . . Chamomile had eaten the whole pile of candy and felt very, very *sick*!

"Oh dear, oh dear!" said the queen, scooping her up gratefully and bundling her home to bed. "But at least now you know."

"Know what?" said Chamomile weakly.

"That candy makes you sick, little madam!" said Nanny Nettle.

"That's why I never allow it."

"You're wrong!" cried Chamomile, throwing back the covers and jumping out of bed. "It wasn't the *candy*. It was *too much* candy—eaten all at once because I was so excited about having what I'm not allowed. *That's* what made me sick! And that's why I rode my bike where I wasn't allowed and got bagged by that bad cat Bags-Eye!"

"Bagged?" gasped the king and queen.

"Yes," said Chamomile. "He was going to send you a ransom note but he couldn't write so I wrote it, and that's how I told you where I was."

"Oh, my goodness!" gasped Nanny Nettle. "What are we going to do with her?"

"I know," said the king. "We're going to give her a little of what she's not allowed!"

"Just a little," said the queen, "so she doesn't want anything so much that it gets her into trouble."

"Jelly mice, I think," said Chamomile.

"And," said the king, "Nanny Nettle is going to take you for a bike ride every day of the week!"

"But I can't ride a bike!" gasped Nanny Nettle.

"Then you'll learn," said the king.

"We'll all learn," said the queen.

So they all learned to ride a bike. And—keeping a careful eye out for that bad cat, Bags-Eye—every day someone took Chamomile for a ride on the wild side of the castle walls.

Every week, Nanny Nettle ordered a few sweets to be delivered from Bulls-Eye the Good Cat's Candy Store in town. And every week, Chamomile counted them out.

When she gave Nanny Nettle her share, she said, "Now don't eat them all at once, Nanny Nettle. You *know* that's not allowed!"